Jimmy is no mind reader. But when he meets Mr Glynn soon after Leaving Cert results are announced he knows exactly how the conversation will go

'Congratulations, Jimmy. Now you'll be free to take the team again.'

'Don't think so, Mr Glynn.'

Mr Glynn and Harry Hennessy are confounded. How can Jimmy give up as manager of Riverside U-12s, the team he has seen develop from kick-and-rush kids to classy footballers capable of having a glory ear?

mmy explains that he has to get a job.

U-12s are less than impressed with the argument.

What can be more important than tball?

Peter Regan

RIVERSIDE

Exit Point

Illustrated by Terry Myler

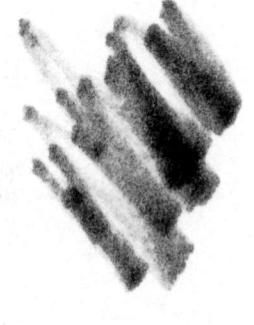

THE CHILDREN'S PRESS

For
Louis Patrick Kellaway

First published 2008 by
The Children's Press
an imprint of Anvil Books
45 Palmerston Road, Dublin 6

1 3 5 6 4 2

© Text Peter Regan 2008
© Illustrations Terry Myler 2008

ISBN 978-1-901737-59-2

Typeset by Computertype Limited
Printed by Colour Books Limited

Contents

1 Cutting Adrift

Early August and Jimmy Quinn feels his life is about to change. There is someone up there directing his every move, making him feel helpless.

I know all this because I am Jimmy Quinn.

All of a sudden my life is racing towards an end and a beginning. Friday I've to go into school for the last time and be handed my Leaving Cert results. I'm not the only one suffering from nerves. There are forty-five of us, the same number as the Dublin to Bray bus. And that could be a lucky omen. For work. It is a tradition for most Bray people to work in Dublin, a lot of whom use the 45 bus as legs to get there.

I'm really looking forward to work. I'll certainly do better on that score than my da. He used to be Ireland's biggest layabout. Then a few things shook him to the core and now he's a Born Again Brick-Layer.

Friday the 13th came and went. I got a good result. So did most of the lads. School was out for the last time.

On the way home Growler Hughes and I bumped into Mr Glynn (the main man at Riverside). I knew exactly what he'd say. In fact, I knew the first two things he'd say, even though I'm no mind reader.

'Lads, how did the exams go?'

'We passed.'

'Congratulations. You'll be free to take the team again, Jimmy?'

'Don't think so, Mr Glynn.'

'Don't let them down, Jimmy. They're depending on you. U-12 is a great age group to manage. I know you had to drop the team last season but you're ready for action again now.'

'Mr Glynn, I've to look for a job. Once I get one I probably won't have the time to manage the team.'

'Think it over.'

'I already have.'

'They're your team, Jimmy. They belong to you.'

Maybe they did belong to me. I'd seen them develop from kick-and-rush eight-year-olds to classy footballers capable of having a glory year at U-12 level. But at that moment in time I didn't see myself having the time to chase after league titles and win cups. I had to do something with my life. It wasn't as if there was no one to take the team. If I gave up I was full certain Mr Glynn and his sidekick Harry Hennessy would take over. I told Mr Glynn as much. I said I'd call around to his house by Tuesday with a final decision.

When I got home everyone was out. I felt slightly disappointed; I wanted to bask in the glory of being the first in the family to pass the Leaving Cert. Instead I went upstairs to the box-room and swung into my secret writing routine. At the time I was working on an article to do with a building development up the town. I just had to put the final touches to it before – hopefully – blasting it into orbit in the *Bray People*.

The article had been on my mind ever since the bulldozers had arrived in the centre of Bray to knock a block of perfectly good shops that had seen a century of satisfied customers to the grave. Property tycoons were behind the scheme. They hoped to make a pile of money.

I got on with my article while waiting for my parents to come home and fill my head with praise over my exam results.

I was looking forward to that and the party the school principal had laid on for later that night.

One certainty: I wouldn't be bringing my da. He could stay home and mind the cat. Though it wasn't really a cat. It was a ferret. But he thought it was a cat, the only one of its kind in Ireland.

2 The Old School

Word wasn't long doing the rounds that I might be giving up the team. Most of the players found it difficult to believe I would walk away and leave them. Some just couldn't understand why I was so hung up on getting a job at all. They were the ones from my side of the tracks where work was something you could take or leave, the latter being the preferred option.

The longest-serving members of the team – Baby Joe McCann, Nobby Roche, Pee Wee Flood and Henry (though he'd defected into Irish dancing) – were convinced I'd sold them down the river.

If only they had known! Inside, I was bleeding. People who have no interest in football will find it impossible to understand how hard it is to walk away from the sport, especially after being so deeply involved. But that's the way it is.

I tried (without success) to explain it to Sheila Murphy, a pretty girl who lived in nearby Greystones. I had met her before the exams and we had gone out a few times. She was a bit of an intellectual, meaning she had brains to burn. By being seen with her I hoped people would think I was also a brainy type. It was time to climb the social and educational ladder.

I brought Sheila with me when I went around to Mr Glynn's house to confirm that I was giving up Riverside to concentrate on making something of my life.

'You sure, Jimmy?'

'Certain.'

'It's sad to see you leave. You know how much we all appreciate what you've done for the club. Any chance of you changing your mind?'

'Mr Glynn, a clean break is the only way.'

'Have you told Harry Hennessy?'

'No, I was hoping you would.'

'Drop by and see him. He'd like to hear first-hand. Jimmy, he always thought the world of you. Okay, in a football sense Chippy was Number One. But as a person, Harry always put you first. You'll get him at home after six.'

It wouldn't be easy telling Harry Hennessy. We all had grown up around Harry. Football was everything to him. It was his life's blood. Just like it had been for me. I could only hope he would understand.

There was something else I had to say.

'Mr Glynn, I hear your Youth team is finished.'

'Not finished, Jimmy. Gone over the age.'

'That's means you've no team to manage. Take over my team as U-12s. That will give you and Harry a new team. You can take them all the way through to Youth level.'

'They won't like the change. They were looking forward to having you back.'

'You've managed them on and off already. A month's time and it will be like you were always there.'

And it probably would. A few months' down the road and they'd have forgotten all about Jimmy Quinn, ex-schoolboy football manager, especially if they were in the hunt for a few trophies. It would be all Harry Hennessy and Mr Glynn then.

Twenty minutes later Sheila Murphy and I were standing outside Harry Hennessy's door. He asked us in. We had a look at some Riverside photos of his, then some of Bray Wanderers, then some of a team called Glenview. When it was all done I broke the bad news. Harry was half expecting it. He didn't say a whole lot except to shake my hand and wish me well. He said he'd organise a get-together with the players so as I could say a last good-bye. I thought that a good idea.

A few minutes later we left Harry Hennessy and went to the library to do some research for my article.

That part of my life was dead as a dodo.

14

Sheila was top-notch at research. She could flick through books at lightning speed and land unerringly on essential nuggets of information. She was also a genius at surfing the internet. I suppose it was one of the reasons I was attracted to her. She was a writer's dream come true. She was my gateway to acquiring knowledge without all the hard brain slog.

What we were looking for now was written proof of what some oul' lad I had met at the building site lately had told me. And in just twenty minutes flat, she had found it.

'It's here, the old school the old man spoke about.'

I looked at the entry. It tied in with what he had said. He had brought me to the site, directly behind where the shops were to be demolished and pointed out the school. It looked derelict and run-down, crying out to be saved. And that's when my interest in it began.

'It says,' continued Sheila, 'it was built by Viscount Powerscourt and opened in 1829 as Bray Infant School. It became Bray Technical

School from 1902 until it closed in 1933.'

'The oul' lad said it was used for meetings after that, and for storing stuff in. His father-in-law went to school there in 1930.'

We stayed there for a further hour and got fresh information. At least Sheila did. I kept busy writing it all down in a jotter. Finished, we went to McDonald's and had a Big Mac.

The oul' lad hadn't just shown me the outside of the sad wreck of the school. He brought me inside and pointed out where his father-in-law used to sit. Only now there were no desks, no seats, no nothing. Only an empty shell, and a loud echoing effect every time we spoke. Then he brought me up a rickety staircase to a small landing.

'Can you reach up there?' he said pointing to a ledge over a doorway.

'Don't think so.'

'Pity.'

'Is there anything I can stand on?'

'I can try and give you a leg-up.'

'You must be joking.'

I went back down the rickety staircase and out to the back, found an empty wooden box and brought it up the stairs. Now I had a bird's eye view of the ledge which was battened over with a dusty length of wood.

'It's hinged. Pull it open.'

I did as he instructed. It was quite shallow inside. There was a faded yellowish length of oilcloth with something wrapped in it.

'It's there, isn't it?' asked the oul' lad.

'There's something all right. What is it?'

'Get it down here. Almost 150 years untouched!'

When I opened the oilcloth there was a further wrapping of a silk-like material. The oul' lad got all excited and insisted on personally opening the silk covering. Inside was a sword in a weathered scabbard.

'Amazing. After all these years ... You say you're against this development?'

'Yes.'

'Would you be prepared to join a campaign to save this old school?'

'Yes.'

'Swear on the sword.'

I thought that was real cool! To swear on the sword that I wanted to save the old school. Like something out of history.

The swearing over, the oul' lad took possession of the sword and scabbard. He said he was bringing them home for safe keeping, that the sword would have a part to play in the campaign. He also told me that there was a great story attached to it that he'd tell me all about it one day soon. Meanwhile he told me to get the word out and start the ball rolling.

'What's your name?' I asked before we split.

'Charles Darley. Captain Charles Darley.'

'An army man?'

'Ex.'

We parted company, the Captain having noted my address.

And that's how my article changed tack. From being an indictment of fat-cat developers (the Captain's words) tearing down familiar landmarks to build faceless blocks it would have a new focus. It would now be a clarion call to preserve our heritage. That call would be:

Save the Old School.

3 Getting Organised

I wasn't the only one making a new start in life. My sister was getting married and we all had to go down to Bantry for the wedding. I invited Sheila along but she said she'd give it a miss. She hadn't much time for my da.

All the relations from Belfast showed up. Usually they went on a week's holiday to Spain but on account of the wedding they had turned family-minded and decided to take in Bantry Bay instead. A busful made the trip. Some were talented drum and flute musicians. Thankfully, they left the instruments at home.

When I got back after the wedding, I kept busy scouring the newspapers for job vacancies and rewriting my article. By now the Captain was in full feather, aflame with the idea of saving the old school. He would, he told me, launch a protest campaign on a 'proper war footing', his first requirement being troops to serve in the trenches. Unfortunately all the ones he knew were long dead, so he sent me to Riverside to muster up a platoon.

'Want to get involved in a protest?' I asked Georgie O'Connor and Ginger Mullin, those two stars – or horrors – of schoolboy football, depending on which angle you were looking at them from.

'No, you walked out on us. We belong to Harry and Mr Glynn now. Get lost!'

Pee Wee Flood, my top-notch goal-scorer, was equally dismissive.

'Save a school! I hate schools. Anyway, you left us high and dry.'

'I didn't. I have to get a job, meaning I haven't time for football. I have to work.'

'Tell me another!'

I didn't bother telling him another. Instead I went on looking for recruits. I didn't give up until I'd gone through the entire squad of what had been my old U-11 team. Not one of them responded to the call. Still it wasn't all doom and gloom. The whole bunch of them called round one night and presented me with a lovely inscribed plaque for all I'd

done for them. It brought tears to my eyes even if it didn't do much for the cause.

When push came to shove all I could muster were a few old pals, namely Growler Hughes, Victor and his brother Henry, and, of course, Flintstone, who by now was into full pedal-power with Bray Wheelers. Two late volunteers were Dan and Illie, the identical Romanian twins, who wanted to join the campaign. But Captain Darley put a damper on them. 'Nice one. But we don't want an International Brigade. The cause is local and will have to remain so.'

Already I could sense that Captain Darley was a man of principle. Growler Hughes preferred to see him as some kind of exotic plant, 'of the fruit and nut variety'. We all knew what he meant.

A few days later, Captain Darley got us all together for a chat on strategy.

'The cornerstone of our campaign,' he boomed, 'has to be a local politician. No local politicians, no campaign. And only one has agreed to help.'

He paused, almost as if to take in air.

We were already on his wavelength. We had a fair idea who that lone politician was.

'Mrs. O'Leary,' he said.

We had got it in one. Mrs O'Leary the scourge of Bray, Mrs O'Leary of the thumping handbag, was to be our champion.

On the plus side, our depleted platoon would soon be reinforced. What with Mrs O'Leary's countless mites of grandchildren certain to join the ranks we'd no longer have a platoon; we'd have a full-sized army.

They had to be a match for the fat-cats.

Long live the Revolution!

4 The Waterloo Sword

In between shooting off letters of application for every kind of job that was going, I worked hell-for-leather revising my article about the old school, checking every morning and afternoon that it was still there and that the bulldozers hadn't smashed it to smithereens. Sheila kept rushing me new morsels of information.

I had already written ten pages of the stuff, much too much for the *Bray People* to print, but I'd do an edit and make it trim and to the point. Captain Darley wanted a sneak preview but I politely told him to get lost. He was now coming to the house most afternoons to give me a progress report. He was turning into a proper nuisance. But he did give me some new information. Over muffins and tea (he brought the muffins) he told me the history of the sword that had been hidden in the old school.

'You must write the history of the sword into the article,' he ordered in true officer-to-private style.

'How can I when you haven't told it to me yet?'

'Well, I'm telling you now. That sword goes back to the Battle of Waterloo. You've heard of the Battle of Waterloo?'

'Course I have. And Waterloo Station in London. I spent a day there with my da looking for Manchester. I was only seven at the time. My da had to do the talking. That's how we got lost.'

'The Battle of Waterloo was fought in 1815 between the British and the French. It was one of the most important battles in history. Napoleon was in charge of the French. The Duke of Wellington led the British forces. By the way, the duke was Irish.'

'If he was Irish what was he doing fighting for Britain?'

'That was the way it was in those days. Remember, Ireland was part of Britain back then. Don't they teach you history at school?'

'I've just left school. Any chance of getting me a job?'

'Could do so. Fancy a career in the Army?'

'No way. I've a few interviews coming up – maybe I'll get an offer. The Army is out though. I'm not into blood and guts.'

But that wasn't entirely the truth. The army the Captain had in mind was the British Army. I'd fall out with most of my pals if I joined the British Army. The only organisation I wanted to join in Britain was Manchester United but I wasn't good enough. Anyway, I knew I would totally fall apart with nerves if I ever got to play in front of a packed stadium at Old Trafford. Thirty of a crowd is my limit. Perhaps I'd do better if I were blind. But then I wouldn't be able to see the ball.

'There's a link between the sword and the school we're trying to save. Both are linked to Bray's old British tradition.'

'What do you mean?'

'In the 1800s Bray was mainly in favour of the link with Britain.'

'Are you sure? I think you're making a mistake?'

'Mistake! It's pure fact!'

I shut up. I'd just remembered that my grandfather had fought in the British Army during the Second World War.

'The sword belonged to a man named Jones. He lived just below Bray bridge and was a topping good assistant to his father who was a blacksmith. In time he joined the Army and fought with distinction at Waterloo. Sadly, he lost a hand in the battle.

'After the war he came home to Ireland and took over his father's forge. In place of his amputated hand he had an iron hook attached. The locals nicknamed him "Iron Fist". Pride of place in the forge was the sword he had carried into battle. After some years it was removed for safekeeping. There were those about the town who regarded the sword as being of an insulting nature. You understand what I'm referring to, don't you?'

I did understand. They were Irish rebels and I was just right with them. But I didn't tell the Captain. I didn't want to hurt his feelings. So I politely told him to get on with the story.

'For fear the disloyal faction would destroy the sword it was taken to the old school and hidden exactly where you took it

from the other day. Yours is one of the few hands to touch it since approximately 1867.'

I liked that. It was the oldest thing I'd ever touched in my life. What an honour — even if all the old-time rebels had hated the sight of it. I had no problem with the sword. It was a part of history and history shouldn't be interfered with. It and the school were linked and both deserved to be looked after.

I was completely taken by Captain Darley. He was a great man to talk. I listened and got it all down on paper. In a week's time I'd be up to the *Bray People* office banging the door down, demanding publication of my article and publicity for the upcoming campaign to save the old school from the fat cats.

A week later I got an offer of a job. It didn't come through post, phone or text. It came by word of mouth. Victor came looking for me and made me an offer I just had to refuse. It was with a firm where he worked himself, part-time so it didn't interfere with his stint in the Chinese restaurant.

'Jimmy, it's not a bad job.'

'Knocking on people's doors selling bibles isn't what I'd call a job. You're dumped on an estate with a load of bibles and have to lug them from door to door. If you don't sell you don't get paid. If it rains you're soaked to the skin and your bibles get all soggy. And if they do you're sacked on the spot and have to make your own way home. And all for peanuts. It's no way to spread the word of God. No thanks.'

'You're right about the rain. I nearly got drenched yesterday only I sheltered under a hedge. I sang a few U2 songs to pass the time. That's the worst of workin' on your own. It's not so bad if you have someone with you. Why not give it a try for a few weeks? If something better crops up you can chuck it in.'

'If it's company you want, go and ask Flintstone.'

Victor did ask Flintstone. The offer was accepted and they spent nine days doing unpaid missionary work on the south side of Dublin. On the ninth day they sat on the bibles and had a heart-to-heart. As the boss (who drove them to the estates and picked them up afterwards) didn't know their home addresses the idea of chucking the job in occurred to them – and they did! They left the bibles and a jumbo bag of sweets as a reward at the pick-up point with two local eight-year-olds. They also left a note for the boss-man explaining they had had enough and that God would understand.

And that was the Gospel, according to SS Flintstone and Victor.

5 The Campaign Gets Under Way

Captain Darley was not a man to let the grass grow under his feet. Almost before I had got my pathetic effort at a platoon assembled than he had hired a hall and called a meeting of all interested parties. The idea was to count heads and plan strategy. Mrs O'Leary was at the top table along with the Captain. They had become firm allies and were all for moving the campaign forward as quickly as possible. Sheila and I were invited to join them, though we didn't speak.

The hall was full. On closer examination it turned out to be mainly full of O'Learys, mostly nippers and diehard teenagers. Flintstone, Growler Hughes, Victor and Henry sat down at the back. They were the only ones there from my Riverside days. I gave them a wave. They waved back. I knew they'd stay with me through thick and thin. We'd give the *Save the Old School* campaign a right go.

Mrs O'Leary spoke first: 'I've approached every councillor in this town to assist in our campaign. But the powers that be don't want to know! When I asked for something to be done I was ignored. But we will rectify the situation. We will make them see the light. The old school should be made a protected building. *Must* be made a protected building.'

'Hear! Hear!'

'So it's up to us to start an active campaign. Protest at every opportunity. Occupy the building site if necessary.'

'Hear! Hear!'

It was the Captain who began the litany of Hear! Hear! Soon enough we were all at it.

'The town is being brought to its knees through incompetence. Years ago a new shopping centre was proposed. What was done? A thirty-foot crater was dug. Then the developers walked away. What was left? An eyesore that rapidly filled with rainwater, a threat to human health and safety. And who complained? *Absolutely no one!* Now it's time to make a stand. To make the old school an issue. To defend the cultural values of this town. We will not back down until we have our way. Enough is enough.'

Every word Mrs O'Leary had said was the truth. Just ask Flintstone and Henry. At first, when the bottom fell out of the proposed new shopping centre and turned into a hole, Flintstone and Henry thought it a good place to go for a swim. So too did the local ducks and swans. But once the water got murky not even the local rats touched it. It became known as 'The Hole in the Ground'. It was a local landmark.

'We need posters to highlight the issue. Who's going to look after that?'

'I will,' volunteered Sheila.

'Posters cost money. You will have to be compensated.'

'Mrs O'Leary, I don't mind.'

'But I do. We'll have to fund-raise. Any ideas out there?'

'I've a capital wheeze,' suggested the Captain. 'What about a gymkhana?'

A look of horror descended over the hall. And it wasn't because those present hadn't got a pony between them. Gymkanas are just not our kind of thing.

'Not practical,' frowned Mrs O'Leary. 'We need something with more popular appeal. Something that can be organised right away.'

'I've got an idea,' piped up Henry from the back of the hall. 'I do Irish dancing. I could do some on the Main Street. I'm sure people would give me money.'

And so they would. Deluge him with it, in fact. Everyone in Bray knew about Henry and his Irish dancing routine. He'd become famous over the last few months. The only snag; the counting would be more tiresome than the dancing.

'We can go along with that. Any more ideas?'

Growler Hughes was on his feet. 'What about a whiparound? We could collect money as people go out.'

But Mrs O'Leary was one for striking when the iron was hot. She seized the tweed golf cap the Captain was wearing, dropped a €20 note (which she held up beforehand) into it and, having received the donations of the Captain (€50) and €10 each from Sheila and myself, removed the money and sent it

on its travels with two small O'Learys. It returned with an extra €24 and eighty cents in two-cent coins.

Every one at the top table had a good idea of where the two-cent coins came from – the little O'Learys. But the nuisance of all the small change would be more than offset by their value once the campaign started. They'd be in the front line screaming their little hearts out for the cause and generally making a nuisance of themselves. O'Learys are something else when it comes to protests. They are born that way.

Everyone over five foot tall was given a job. Sheila was to to look after the posters. Growler after the money. The older O'Learys were assigned to paste up the posters, with supervision by Flintstone, Victor and Henry.

'Jimmy,' said Mrs O'Leary. 'You will be in charge of publicity, public relations...that sort of thing. By the way – how's the article getting on?'

Thanks to the Captain, it was now common knowledge.

She herself undertook to look after getting sponsorship around the town. As did the Captain; he said he'd organise a collection among his few remaining pals from the time they were in the Boys' Brigade.

The main point for discussion was: When would the protests begin?

There wasn't much argument. With the bull-dozers breathing down the backs of our collective necks, it obviously had to be as soon as possible.

So the decision was made to hold it in four days' time, It was to be a lightning strike, held at the junction where the site met the Main Street. That meant traffic disruption, ensuring that plenty of people would see us. We were to make up our own posters for the day. Thereafter, proper placards, designed and made by Sheila, would be available.

It was agreed Mrs O'Leary wouldn't attend the first protest. She would be held back to fight the cause in the council chamber and for the later stages of the campaign. She was to be our special weapon and would only be used on important days

The day after the meeting I was invited to Mrs O'Leary's house to show her and the Captain the finished article for the *Bray People*. They both liked what they read and praised my writing skills, saying my style was like that of a a young Ernest Hemingway. I hadn't a clue who he was except that Sheila told me he was a dead American and that some of his books had been turned into films.

Afterwards Mrs O'Leary brought me to the *Bray People* office where she asked for the editor. We were directed upstairs to an office where he sat gazing into the silver haze of a computer monitor.

He didn't gaze for long. Mrs O'Leary took over and told him all about the article I had just written and the campaign to save the old school.

' When is it due to be knocked?' he asked.

'Within three weeks. We need action and fast.'

'I'll send a photographer to your protest,' he said to her. To me, he said, 'I'll read the article over the week-end. Get back to me first thing Monday morning. I'll give a decision whether to publish, or not, then.'

We left.

The campaign had begun.

We'd see it through.

6 The First Protest

On the day of the first protest we were in fine fettle. Our spirits were buoyed by the news that Henry had attracted hordes of shoppers and raised €200 for the campaign. Luckily the day was sunny.

Only downside was that the police moved him on, saying he hadn't a permit to collect money and that he was obstructing the footpath. There was also a problem with the noise level of the Irish music blaring from his ghetto-blaster. Henry took it all to heart and began to cry, so one of the policemen helped to dry his tears and took him and his dancing-shoes home in a squad car.

The fine sunny weather continued on for the protest. A good crowd, definitely sixty, turned out, even if half were nippers. Most of us carried home-made placards:

Shame!
Save our Heritage!
Hands off the Old School!
Money Destroys!

We had gathered in a laneway about a minute's march from where the builders were hell-bent on obliterating the old school and our 'glorious past'. Growler and I were early and we went over to the building site to have a look. The front part had been completely levelled and there was a huge crater in the ground. Heavy machinery was loading the clay and debris into lorries, enlarging the crater to make the under-round car park even more enormous. At the back of the site stood the old school. That part hadn't been interfered with yet.

I hadn't had much of a look around the place the time the Captain showed me the sword. But this time I noticed a nice circular window in the gable-end. There was also a crest but it was hard to make out. Only the number '1829' stood out. I remembered that the Captain had said that was the year the school was built.

'You see those two buildings beside it?' said Growler. I nodded

'One was a sausage factory, the other made fire-extinguishers. They were built much later.'

'Which was the sausage factory?'

'Darned if I know. All I know is that my grand-dad went to school here when it was a technical school.'

'He couldn't have gone to it any earlier,' I said. 'It was built as a school for the likes of the Captain's crowd. You had to have a British pedigree to go there.'

'Why are we saving it then?'

'Everything was built by the British then. Except mud-walled cottages.'

'Oh!'

We didn't hang around for long. We didn't want the builders to notice us and think we were snooping. We wanted to take them by surprise when the protest started.

As we waited back in the lane it began to dawn on us that we hadn't got a leader. The Captain hadn't shown up!

Panic set in!

'He's done a runner!'

'He's all puff and wind.'

'Give him another few minutes.'

'Maybe with all the excitement he's dropped dead of a heart attack.'

'We'll go ahead without him.'

40

'Who's going to act as leader?'

'I will.'

Of course, it was Growler Hughes who had leaped into the breach. He told us to line up in rows and march on the site, just the way the Captain would have wanted it.

'Pity I haven't got a megaphone. I'd give those builders a right earful.'

We trooped from the lane and were within 200 yards of the building site when who should come along, dressed in some old-day military uniform, only the Captain. He looked the picture of an officer all dressed up to dash off to a cavalry charge at the Battle of Waterloo. To underline the point he had the sword in its scabbard all neatly in place by his side.

Soon as I saw his rig-out I knew there would be trouble.

He took command at the head of the mob.

'Not a word. Head straight for the old school. We'll take it by storm. Follow me!'

We got to the school before the builders knew what was going on. Once there we opened up with a barrage of slogans and protests. The Captain was to the fore. He positioned us all around the school, making sure we had our placards slogan-side out.

Two building workers wearing safety gear were standing around having a cup of tea. They looked alarmed, dropped their tea and ran down into the crater at the front of the site, where the excavating for the underground car park was going on. They came back with some of the work crew. We were told to clear off or the police would be called.

By now Growler Hughes had got into the school, gone up the rickety staircase and got out on the roof through a skylight. He stood upright and waved an Irish tricolour.

'Look, Captain, look! I'm claiming the school for Ireland.'

The Captain's retort was quick: 'That's not my flag! But by God it will do!'

With that he drew the sword from the scabbard and held it above his head.

'Charge!'

Suiting action to work, he charged at the building workers, probably in much the same way as 'Iron Fist' Jones had at the Battle of Waterloo. He probably thought we were behind him, galloping the legs off our

imaginary horses. But, in truth, we were too much in fear of the building workers, even though they were now fleeing, to move a step. We stood rooted to the spot. That's except for Growler up on the roof.

'Go get them, Captain!' he roared.

But the Captain only charged as far as the edge of the crater. He knew better than to rush down the clay slope after the stamped-ing workers for fear of being ambushed. He could see some were using mobile phones, no doubt ringing for the police. He sheathed the sword and came back to us. If we ever needed proof of the Captain being totally barmy we had it now.

'Guerilla tactics!' boomed the Captain. 'Throw away the placards and disperse. Each man for himself. No two together. Melt into the landscape. You, up on the roof, make a run for it and take that infernal flag with you. We don't want anyone taken prisoner.'

'Captain, why did you have to use the sword?' asked an ashen nine-year-old.

'Use the sword? I'd never! I was only pretending. Luckily it worked – shock tactics and all that.'

The Captain saluted, turned and rushed through a hinged door built into some hoarding just behind the old school. There was a builder's sign pasted to the door. It read: **Exit Point**.

The rest of us left by way of the main site entrance, the same way we had come in, and scattered. We knew the place would fill with squad cars and police within minutes. The plan now was not to get caught, and we didn't.

Unknown to us the photographer from

44

the *Bray People* arrived minutes after we left the site. She introduced herself to the building workers. They told her to get lost. Then the police introduced themselves to her. Lucky for us she told them to get lost.

The 'Phantom Army' had struck its first blow.

We'd be back!

7 Growler Gets Big Ideas

Things were pretty static on the jobs front. All my applications seemed to have ended in waste bins. Then, on the Monday after the protest, I noticed a letter lying on the floor in the hall; it had floated through the letterbox and made a soft landing. It wasn't the usual bill. It was addressed to me personally. From some company I'd never heard of, asking me to attend for interview the following week. They were looking for sales staff of the door-to-door variety to sell directories.

After what had happened with Victor and Flintstone and the bibles, I tore up the letter and threw it into the bin. As if to rub in the kind of junk jobs I was being offered, soon as I had binned it who came knocking on the door but Growler.

'Have a look at these,' he said pulling two fancy envelopes from his pocket. 'They're from banks. I've been asked to go for interviews. No dead-end jobs for me.'

Sure enough, the letters were from two top-notch banks. They were always on TV.

'*Let us make you a fortune!*', '*Invest with us and change your life!*'. All that kind of blarney. I couldn't see them investing in Growler. Not if they met him face to face.

'How did you pull it off? All I'm getting are crumby offers from no-hopers.'

'Simple! You have to have the right address. Then you get the right job offers.'

'What do you mean?'

'Look at the address on the envelopes.'

'That's not where you live.'

'Good address though. It's Patrick's. He told me to use it.'

Patrick was Growler's new pal. His da is a millionaire and lives at one of the best addresses in Bray. At one time Patrick was addicted to wearing disguises and going to receptions where there was plenty of free sandwiches and bottles of wine, but Growler had cured him and now they were best pals.

'Get an address like that and you'll have plenty of job offers.'

'What if someone finds you out?'

'Once you're in the job a few months you tell them you've moved to a new address. They'll never find out.'

'With a bit of luck! Are you going for the interviews?'

'Of course! I've all me best clothes laid out. I'll sail through the interviews.'

I doubted it. He'd sail into a hurricane.

You see, Growler has trouble with sums. His addition and subtraction are shaky. His multiplication is guesswork and his division is a pious hope.

I didn't want to depress him but I thought I ought to warn him.

'Growler,' I began, 'do you think your maths are up to it? These jobs are about banking. Money. High finance. You must be able to calculate things.'

He put his arm on my shoulder in his best Humphrey Bogart manner.

'Jimmy, old son,' he said in that soothing voice you reserve for half-wits. 'Do you know anything about banking?'

Before I could open my mouth and prove that I didn't, he went on, 'Banking isn't like it was in the old days. Rows of fellows sitting on high stools totting up ledgers. And telling you they couldn't lend you any money. That you were a bad risk. That's all gone out the window. No, banking is now a creative career. You see, everyone wants money … *and the banks have money.* So you lend them money and you make a huge profit when they repay it.'

I wasn't quite following this.

'Suppose they don't repay it?'

'They don't have to. The bank sells on the debt to someone else.'

'A bad debt.'

'Jimmy, you don't call it a bad debt. You call it a bond or a hedge fund or a credit swap. And the fellas who make the loans get millions in bonuses. I think I'm going to be very good at that kind of thing.'

I hadn't time to stay talking to him. Tell him he'd got something wrong somewhere along the line. I'd just remembered that I had to be at the *Bray People*.

At the *Bray People* I was ushered into the editor's office. His name was Fred.

'Take a seat. Jimmy isn't it?'

'Yes.'

'Too sunny to be stuck in an office but that's the nature of the business. I know you from somewhere. Your face looks familiar.'

'Don't think so.'

'You run a football team out of Bray Park.'

'I've given it up. I'm looking for a job.'

'Just out of school?'

'Yeah. I finished in June.'

'Did you do your Leaving Cert?'

'Just got the results. I passed.'

'Good for you. That article you wrote on the old school. I like it…but…'

He took it from a drawer and laid it on the desk. I knew he was getting ready to hand it back and, politely, show me the door. My heart sank quicker than the *Titanic.*

'The article is interesting. But the subject matter is too contentious.'

I knew what contentious meant. It meant **trouble**.

'Building developments are needed in this town. The powers-that-be want this project to go ahead. We can't afford to have another failed venture. End up with another hole in the ground. If we were to support your campaign, we'd be stepping on too many toes. So I have to turn your article down.'

'But what about the old school?'

50

'What about it? There are other buildings that are far more worth saving. I appreciate your zeal. But you will have to run on your own with this one.'

When I first entered the room I thought he was a nice man. Now I was beginning to think differently. Newspaper editors should be defending old buildings, not turning a blind eye and allowing them to be knocked down. Heritage should be preserved, not destroyed! I was going to tell him so but he was talking again.

'There's another point. We sent a photo-

51

grapher along to the site the other day. She arrived slightly late. But she saw enough. She says there was a disturbance. Led by some unbalanced person dressed in old military style carrying a sword and raving on about the might of Empire. Is he a looney? ... Jimmy, as a responsible paper we have to strike a balance between preservation and progress. See both sides. I hope you understand.'

He handed me back my article. I was totally gutted. I had given it my all. And now in the space of ten minutes I was on the verge of failure.

'There's something else.'

'What?'

'There's potential in your writing. Ever think of making writing a career?'

Of course I had thought of it. Apart from football it was all I thought of morning, noon and night.

'We have a job vacancy. Junior reporter. Mainly reporting the local soccer scene. What do you think?'

What did I think?

From being gutted, I was gobsmacked!

'It would involve a course in journalism at Rathmines College. Part work, part study effort. Of course you'd be on a salary and we'd look after your fees. Think it over.'

I didn't need to think it over. It was my dream come true. A potential journalist! Maybe a top reporter trawling Bray for news scoops. The *Bray People* editor shot to dizzying heights in my esteem. As for the old school, it would have to look after itself. Maybe he was right. Maybe it wasn't all that important. Except to the Captain, that is.

'I'll give you a few days. Come back next Thursday week; we can talk it over then.'

I mumbled thanks, left the office over-joyed and headed home. Mrs O'Leary could wait until tomorrow to get the news that the article had been turned down by the *Bray People*. I had more important matters on my mind – like being a fully-fledged newspaper reporter!

Thanks to me the Quinns were finally coming up in the world.

I'd put them on the map!

8 Return to Riverside

For fear the job offer with the *Bray People* might fall through I didn't say a word to anyone. But I had to tell Mrs O'Leary that the *Bray People* weren't going to back the campaign. I thought she'd fly into a rage and whirl her handbag over her head like a windmill gone out of control. But she didn't. She was quite calm. Almost as if she knew in advance that it was a non-runner. Somebody had told her about Captain Darley chasing the workers around the site with a sword held at arm's length.

'He shouldn't have done that,' she sighed. 'A sword is an offensive weapon. It's an offence to even carry such a weapon. And to use it to chase people is asking for a prison sentence. Good job the police weren't there at the time. I have had a word with Captain Darley and put him in his place. Either the sword goes or he goes.'

'What did he say?'

'The sword goes.'

'He is very fond of that sword.'

'I met him halfway. He can bring it to committee meetings. Such a man! I don't know where they got him from.'

'Probably the British Empire.'

'By the way, your girl-friend Sheila has completed the official placards for the protests. From now on I'll be directing every protest in person. After what happened we can't trust the Captain. I will be in sole charge.'

I was delighted to have the latest update on the situation.

Firstly, it was nice to hear Mrs O'Leary refer to Sheila as my girl-friend. Officially, we weren't a total item, not yet. Though I thought I had spent enough money on her to qualify, bringing her to the pictures and up to the fancy Chinese restaurant where Victor worked. Maybe after the campaign we'd officially become boy-friend and girl-friend.

Secondly, it was good that the Captain and his sword wouldn't be leading any more protests. The campaign would have floundered with him at the helm. Not only that; we'd probably have become the protest with the greatest number of followers sent to prison at the one time. We'd have made headline news in the media, probably got into the *Guinness Book of Records*.

Mrs O'Leary had averted all that. The Captain had been demoted.

That Saturday I went down to the People's Park, Riverside Boys home ground. I carried a pen and notebook in an inside pocket. I was on a secret mission – to try out reporting, just in case the proposed job with the *Bray People* turned up trumps. There was no point getting all excited about a job I found I couldn't do; I wanted to find out in advance if I could. I wouldn't say a word. Just take out pen and notebook on the sly and record the match. Good reporters write from notes.

I got to the game before the kick-off. The opposition was Cherry Orchard, a top-notch team from Dublin, and, boy, did they know it. It showed in the way they swaggered around the place before kick-off. They were tickled pink by the strangeness of it all.

'It's real country. Look at them trees over

there. They're higher than the houses.'

'Must have been part of a forest once. Bet the ground is all humps and bumps. It's a disgrace asking us to play here.'

'And the mountains. They're almost on the pitch. I hope we're not playing against a crowd of mountainy men. They'll kick us all over the place.'

'Not the way we play football. If we don't beat them by six goals I'll throw me boots in that river over there. They probably swim in it after matches. Probably the only bath they get.'

'Donkeys bray, don't they? That must be how the place got its name.'

'Whatever about donkeys, I can smell pig. Yuk!'

'Better be careful. They might hear us. And act up nasty. They could be a bunch of locos.'

Luckily none of the Riverside players heard the comments but I did. I felt hurt. I felt like having it out with the sneerers. The People's Park and Riverside meant so much to me. But I held my peace.

Seeing my old team run out on to the pitch

made me feel emotional. Too many good memories flooded my mind. But I reminded myself of what I was doing there, that I was attempting to report on a football match and convince myself that I was capable of doing the job.

The team was exactly as I would have picked it and the match got off to a flier. Pee Wee Flood caught the Cherry Orchard defence cold from a cross. The keeper came out but Pee Wee deftly headed the ball into the empty net. Riverside were 1-0 up.

Cherry Orchard continued to strut their stuff, lording the game with classy inter-passing and long spells of possession. But Mr Glynn and Harry Hennessy had Riverside well prepared. They mostly relied on playing the midfield very tight, with the wide men covering back and closing down the spaces inside their own half. Cherry Orchard found it hard to offset Riverside's blanket defence and get in on goal. Any shot that did get through was comfortably dealt with by goal-keeper Nobby Roche. Dave Doherty and Baby Joe McCann organised the defence brilliantly. And the midfield weren't half bad. In fact, the whole team was brilliant. They looked very good under new management.

Though I'd be slow to admit it, Mr Glynn and Harry Hennessy had much more experience in the management stakes than I had. For organisation and strategy they couldn't be faulted. They had the team playing really well. And they lasted the pace. Though Cherry Orchard did strike back with a headed goal near the end, the game finished in a 1-1 draw. Not a bad result, especially against one of the best teams in the Dublin Schoolboys League.

I thought I'd get out of the Park without any fuss. But soon as the game ended the players surrounded me like bees around a hive. They thanked me for showing up, said it was a nice gesture and wished me luck. I began to feel sad again but I didn't let it show.

'What was with the pen and paper?' asked Georgie O'Connor. 'I saw you scribblin' down stuff during the match.'

'Yeah, what's with the notebook?' asked Ginger Mullin. 'Hope you're not spyin' for

some other team.'

'No, nothing like that. Just some project I'm working on.'

'Will you be down to see us again?' queried Baby Joe McCann. 'You could become a fan.'

'Don't think so. Then I don't know.'

And I was telling the truth. More than likely if I became a soccer reporter I would be in the Park again. Time would tell.

Then Mr Glynn came over.

'Hi, Jimmy.'

'Hi, Mr Glynn.'

'I'd like to thank you for leaving us with such a strong squad. Pity you can't be around to reap the rewards. They're a fine bunch, full of skill and effort. They just love their football. Thanks to you.'

'I wouldn't say that, Mr Glynn. Harry and you are doing a great job. You'll bring them to the next level.'

'We plan to keep them right through to Youth football. From now on, the only worry is whether Dan and Illie will be around to see it all through.'

'What do you mean, Mr Glynn?'

Dan and Illie were identical Romanian twins. At one time they were my aces in the pack when the going got tough.

'Being foreign there's always the chance they may not stay in Ireland. I wouldn't like to lose them. Who knows? But at present that's our only worry.'

Mr Glynn need not have worried. Dan and Illie stayed put in Bray. Dan even went on to play for Bray Wanderers in the Eircom League.

Then Mr Glynn asked me how Chippy was doing.

'I don't know, Mr Glynn. Haven't heard a whisper. No one has.'

'If you hear let me know.'

'I will, Mr Glynn. Thanks for everything.'

With that, I went home to write up the report before my memory went dead.

9 The Interview

I did hear about Chippy – the following day. I knew he had been in trouble with his club, Forest Albion. He had broken club rules by setting up a five-day 'Samba Soccer' school in Bray during the summer, been found out and demoted to training with the reserve team. But another two weeks and the punishment would end and Chippy could take up where he had left off: trying to get on the first-team squad and aim at making it as a professional footballer.

Who told me all this? His mother. I met her when I was out buying a Lotto ticket. Seemingly he had been ringing home with hard-luck stories.

'That's the only time he rings, when he's in trouble.'

I wasn't surprised. I'd often thought the same thing myself. My life was full of Chippy's hard-luck stories. I told his ma he'd get over it, bade her good day and headed off scratching the Lotto card.

I had lost yet again.

Thursday of that week was a red-letter day. Two meetings! In the morning I was to go to the *Bray People* office to see if I would get the job as junior reporter. That evening there was a meeting to do with the *Save the Old School* campaign.

Of the two, the *Bray People* meeting was by far the most important to me. Yet I was slightly dreading it.

On the way to their office I met Victor and Henry. Lately Victor had ambitions of being a chef. First step was to graduate to doing chicken curries in the takeaway section of his Chinese restaurant. Then hopefully he'd get to cook five-course meals for set dinners. It was the sum total of Victor's ambitions, that and roaming the countryside with his camcorder.

He had just bought some football magazines for Henry. Henry, who had once played on my U-10 football team, had given up football for Irish dancing. But now it seems he was feeling lonesome for football again. He didn't want to make a comeback with Riverside but Victor felt the magazines would help to fill a void. The worse thing about football is that it gets into the blood. It's very hard to walk away from. Once a football fan always a football fan. Some people call fans 'football nutters'.

'Where you off to?'

'The *Bray People*, Victor.'

'We'll go with you.'

'I've a meeting.'

'We'll wait outside.'

'I could be a while.'

'We'll hang on.'

I didn't want them waiting. If the meeting was to be drawn out they'd probably come barging in and tell me to hurry up, maybe spoiling my chance of landing the job. Maybe when the editor saw Victor and Henry he'd have second thoughts and withdraw the offer; Victor and Henry weren't exactly your pillars of society. So I told them about the job. They had thought the meeting was to do with obtaining publicity for the *Save the Old School* campaign. But when I told them what was at stake they said there was no way they'd go in and spoil my chances of becoming a junior soccer reporter.

In the editor's office, Fred, a mobile phone in one hand, was referring to some article he had on the desk before him. He nodded for me to sit down.

He was doing plenty of tough talking. The vibes were he would be a hard boss to work for. The checking and changes to the article went on for a full five minutes before he was satisfied. Finally, he finished and turned to me.

'If there's one thing certain about the newspaper business it's that it's uncertain. You have to cope with everything…. Tell me, how good is your knowledge of the local soccer scene?'

'Top notch.'

'What contacts do you have within the game?'

'What do you mean?'

'Access to managers and club secretaries. Perhaps Bray Wanderers at senior level.'

'I know them all.'

'League secretaries?'

'I know where to go.'

'Good. Knowing people is everything in this business. We'd like you to take Gaelic football on board too – underage stuff. Do you know enough about the game?'

'Yes, plenty.'

'Rugby? What have you got on rugby?'

'I don't know the first thing about the game.'

'There's not much to be reported anyway. Our main sports reporter covers senior and junior games. It's just the underage stuff.'

'I could learn.'

'I'll get the main sports reporter to fill you in. How's that so far?'

'Fine.'

'Still want the job?'

'Of course.'

'The wages will be scaled, meaning your starting point will be low. But with experience and eventual qualifications that will rise substantially.'

'What do I start with and where do I finish?'

The editor scribbled a few figures and pushed the note-pad in my direction.

'Regarding where you finish that's entirely up to yourself. You can either stay, or use us as a stepping-stone to other job opportunities in journalism.'

'When do I start?'

'Next Monday. Nine-thirty. Sharp. One of the reporters will take you under his wing. There's nothing to be afraid of. Once you are prepared to listen and study it will all happen in its own time....One other point. No more work on that article about the old school. Is that understood?'

'Yes.'

'I don't want that project mentioned in this office. And I don't want to see you involved in the campaign. It's a lost cause.'

'Sure.'

I left the *Bray People* office in something of a daze. Victor and Henry were still outside so I told them the job was mine but to say nothing, not yet. They promised not to mention a word.

'Not until after next Monday.'

'Why?'

'That's when I start work.'

I went down to the seafront for a while to calm down. Victor and Henry came with me. I bought them a candyfloss each. It had become something of a ritual for a few of us

Riverside players to go down to the seafront at high points and low points in our lives. It seemed to put things into perspective.

Then I remembered I was to ring Sheila on her mobile to tell her how I got on. I went to a phone-box, made the call and gave her the good news. She didn't seem in the slightest interested though I didn't read anything into it at the time.

My ma was delighted with the news. So was my sister Fiona, the one who was still at home. When the da came in we told him. He wasn't exactly overjoyed; seemed he was afraid I'd write bad things about him. But when I explained I was to be a sports reporter he relaxed. He wanted to know what sports I'd be reporting on. When I told him football he asked what about horse-racing? 'Pity,' he added. 'I could have given you a hand.'

Thank God for small mercies!

Afterwards I went upstairs and took stock of my clothes. I realised I hadn't got what would befit a sports reporter. First thing next morning I'd go to the Credit Union and withdraw some savings. Then I'd buy a proper sports reporter's outfit. I wanted to look the part.

Before that there was the meeting at eight o'clock sharp to do with the *Save the Old School* campaign. Come seven I got ready and went up the town to find out what Mrs O'Leary and the Captain had in mind.

One certainty: I would be keeping a very low profile. I didn't want to lose my job before I had got it!

10 A Little Night Music

There were a few surprises in store at the
Save the Old School campaign meeting. The
Captain hadn't brought the sword. Neither
was he wearing his Battle of Waterloo
uniform. He came straight from doing some
gardening, with a mix of weeds and leaf
stains on his sleeves.

I explained to Mrs O'Leary that rather
than joining them at the top table, I would
like to sit with my girl-friend in the body of
the hall. She beamed her approval but Sheila
was less cordial. She was ensconsed at the
back with four of the weirdest-looking
weirdos on Planet Earth. They all wore
black, with silver studs on the tips of their
noses, white makeup and black lipstick.
Sheila looked like a fully-fledged vampire
on the batter, maybe even a bat from Hell. It
came as a complete shock to me. I never
knew Sheila was into that kind of carry-on.

I had a word with her before the meeting
began. But it was only a waste of space. She

wanted me to sit with them and forever after dress like them. I told her 'No' and went to another row. What it would mean for our friendship I could only guess. I was so upset I hardly spoke for the entire meeting. Not that I wanted to, but I wouldn't have been able to. I just sat and stared into space.

The first surprise of the night was that was everyone seemed to know about the *Bray People* job. When Mrs O'Leary heard about it she wanted me to make sure the campaign got mega publicity. I had to point out that (a) I wasn't working there yet and (b) I would be in the sports department.

The main topic on the agenda was the next march. The final decision was that we were to meet at the laneway beside the building site at 4 pm the following Monday. Placards were to be provided courtesy of Sheila and her crew. Mrs O'Leary would be in total charge. And the Captain was to leave all military emblems, including the sword, at home.

I wasn't long finding out the identity of the snitch who had betrayed the news about my new job. It wasn't Victor or Henry. It was

Sheila Murphy! She had broadcast the news I had told her in confidence. She seemed to resent the fact that I had got a job and called me a Capitalist Pig!

After the meeting I kept clear of Sheila and her pals from Hell. But as I was leaving the hall I was joined by Captain Darley and Growler Hughes. I wasn't exactly over the moon to see either of them but little did I realise that they had a hidden agenda:

Revolution!

When we left the hall Growler turned *up* Main Street, which was odd. The way home was down the street, not up. At first I thought we were walking Captain Darley home. But when we ended up around the corner from the building site I knew there was something sinister afoot.

'That infernal woman thinks she is running the show but I know to the contrary,' muttered Captain Darley. 'This campaign calls for ingenuity.'

We had gone into a narrow cul-de-sac directly at the back of the old school. In it was one of the smallest and strangest-looking cars I had ever seen. It was like a bubble on wheels. There were no doors as such. Instead the bubble opened sideways, hinge-like. There was barely enough room for the driver and a small-sized passenger inside. I remembered seeing a picture of one once. It was called the 'bubble' car, all the rage in the 1960s and long since disappeared into history.

The Captain lifted up the front of the bubble and took two small packages from the car.

'You checked for a night watchman?' he asked Growler.

'They don't have one. The place is a piece of cake.'

'Prepare to proceed.'

My blood ran cold. The packages were probably bombs! Captain Darley intended to blow up the bulldozers and other earth-moving equipment on the building site!

I could see the headlines:

Bray People **reporter**
blows up new shopping centre

And I had, just that morning, promised the

editor I wasn't going to have anything to do with the campaign.

There was no way I was going in! I'd wait outside. Maybe do a runner down the road before the police arrived on the scene.

The Captain turned to the makeshift door in the hoarding in front of the site and opened it with a key he produced.

Growler was obviously part of the plot. Soon as Captain Darley unlocked the door he walked through, the two packages at the ready.

'Aren't you coming?' the Captain asked me.

I hesitated. 'I'll keep nix.'

'Good thinking! What's the warning signal?'

'Three blasts on a whistle.'

'You've got a whistle?'

'Yes, a football whistle.'

'Never thought of having a watch-out. Clever young chap. What's this your name is?'

'Jimmy…Jimmy.'

Wild horses weren't going to drag my second name out of me.

'Bringing a whistle shows great initiative.'

I followed Captain Darley inside the door just to give the impression I was full of zeal for the cause. As I turned to go back out I noticed the sign pinned to the door: **EXIT POINT.** My mind flashed back to the last protest when the Captain, sword in hand, had rushed through it and made a spectacular disappearance. That was how he had made his escape — through the door and away to safety in his bubble car. The Captain was a smart oul' fox, smarter than I previously thought. He had covered his options in advance!

I was waiting in the cul-de-sac for the longest ten minutes of my life, trying to hide behind a bush and thinking up likely stories for being there at all. I half expected to hear explosions but there was no sound except for the pounding of my heart.

When the ten minutes were up Captain Darley and Growler came back out.

'How did it go?'

'Like clockwork.'

'I didn't hear any explosions.'

'There won't be any.'

'What do you mean?'

'I'll explain later.'

Then Captain Darley squeezed himself into his bubble car, gave us a wave and drove off.

On the way home Growler explained what had been happening.

What a relief! I was in the clear as far as my new job was concerned.

About three o'clock in the morning all the fun began, just like Growler told me it would. What I thought were bombs were small transistors with timing devices attached. They were set to turn on and off for five minutes at a time between three and four o'clock am. There were pre-recorded cassettes in the transistors. Only there wasn't music on the cassettes.

First there was a slow repetition of someone hammering nails. Then it stopped. Two minutes later it started again, only this time more rapidly. It sounded like a cross between Woody Woodpecker going rat-a-tat-tat and a steamroller grinding rocks. Gradually it was replaced by the sound of doors slamming. More silence followed. Then came the ferocious sound of an angle-grinder. That was the worst.

The fact that it was all happening in the early hours of the morning made it sound all the louder. The people living around the site – and there were plenty of them – were slowly being driven mad. The hullabaloo went on for three nights before the Captain sneaked back and removed the transistors from their hiding-places. They had been so well camouflaged that even the building workers had not been able to source them.

The Captain had pulled off a master-stroke. The developers were in everyone's bad books. Complaints flooded in. Mrs O'Leary's protest for Monday couldn't have been better timed. But would it do anything to save the old school?

The developers had a head start.

They had planning permissions and demolition orders.

11 Exit Sheila

I had had second thoughts about Sheila. I rang her on Friday, asked her could we meet and try and sort things out? She agreed. Told me to get the 84 bus to Greystones and she'd be down at the harbour.

On the way to Greystones I imagined Sheila as she had been when I first met her, the fresh sea breeze trailing her auburn hair in the sparkling sunlight. What I got was Sheila in her Dracula gear: coal-black hair, chalk-white face, dark lipstick and a few extra studs.

We walked along the pier and had a chat. Most of it was small talk, that's until we got to the nitty-gritty.

'All my life I've had to wear a school uniform,' she grouched. 'Now it's time to rebel. My friends feel the same way. Don't you?'

'Not really.'

'What do you mean?'

I knew only too well what I meant. I was

to start work with the *Bray People* on Monday morning. What if I showed up dressed like Dracula? I'd be fired, if not on the spot, definitely by lunch hour. Anyway, I didn't want to dress like Dracula. The very thought gave me the creeps. I told her so.

'If that's the way you feel it's all off between us. We've nothing in common. There's no point in going together.'

I understood her reasoning. The girl I wanted to know was Sheila Murphy, but she wanted to be *'Sheila the Vampire'*. Our brief romance was over. As far as I was concerned, she could keep her Dracula outfit, go find herself a witch's broom and fly all the way to the moon.

So we parted. I resisted a final crack; that I hadn't known it was Halloween and that that was why I hadn't brought her any apples or nuts.

Twenty minutes later I was on the bus back to Bray. I went into my favourite drapery shop and bought the most respectable trousers, jacket and shirt on view. If nothing else I'd be the best-dressed junior soccer reporter on the *Bray People.*

I didn't bother telling Flintstone or Victor or Growler Hughes about Sheila. They'd find out quickly enough, especially when they saw her parading around Bray in her scary-looking gear. I would disown her, telling everyone I hadn't a clue who she was, denying point-blank that we'd ever gone round together. I was certainly glad Chippy was away in England honing his football skills. He'd really have put the boot in and spread the news that I'd been stupid enough to get involved with one of the 'Seven Brides of Dracula'.

Chippy has a talent for slagging.

That night the curse of Dracula kicked in. I never felt so depressed in my life. Fresh waves of doubt swept over my mind. Would I be able for the job? I couldn't get away with using a pen and notebook. I'd have to use a computer. But I wasn't able to use a computer! Still, they'd probably teach me. But what if it turned out I was so stupid I couldn't learn? I'd be shown the door, and my name would be muck. Talk about being branded a chip off the old block! I'd never get another job. Well, not a proper one anyway. I could end up being just like my da. What a disaster!

Just when I thought I couldn't cope any more Growler Hughes knocked on the door. He had a suggestion to make.

'Let's sneak out in the dead of night, three o'clock, go up near the old school and play those tapes again. I have them here.'

Growler was getting to be a real pain in the neck.

'No, I can't. I've some work to do. Get Flintstone.'

'There's no point in asking Flintstone. You know why?'

Of course I knew why!

Flintstone was afraid of real dead-of-the-night dark. He went sleep-walking one night and woke up in a pitch-black field sur-rounded by monsters. Only he found out next day that the monsters were cows. But the damage was done and that's why Flintstone is terrified of total darkness. He just wasn't into going walkabout at three in the morning.

'Get Victor,' I said.

Before he took himself off, Growler said he had a favour to ask. I couldn't believe what it was. He, too, was on a test run for his job. He wanted me to let him try out my da for what he called a 'sub-prime' loan. So as he could turn up for his interviews with a prospect in the bag, on the 'Here's-one-I-baked-earlier' lines.

I couldn't wait until I'd got him on the other side of the door, with a snarled warning never to darken it again. Dangling a couple of hundred thousand euros in front of my da would be like asking him if he

wanted a winning Lotto ticket.

Growler got in a parting shot. 'Jimmy, I don't think your heart is in our campaign any more.'

There was a bit about the second visitation of The Noise by Night on local radio next day. The police had found a cap on the site. One of them said he knew who it belonged to.

Growler wasn't wearing a cap. Victor was.

It could have been mine. I could have gone down in family history as having lost a job two days before I'd started it.

Growler was out from now on.

12 Chippy Makes the Small Print

I had planned to have a lie-in Saturday morning but Ginger Mullin came calling. My mother woke me and said Ginger was downstairs with his football kit in a bag. I went down.

'I'm late for the match. They've gone without me.'

'What match?'

'Ballybrack Boys. How will I get there?'

'It's nothing to do with me. I'm not your manager. Mr Glynn is.'

'He's not here. They've all gone off in the minibus. Know how I'll get there?'

'Ballybrack is only four miles. Get a bus.'

'I haven't got the fare. Give's the fare.'

'I don't see why I should.'

'I joined Riverside because of you. You're a mate. Give's the fare.'

And he *had* joined Riverside because of me. I had persuaded him and his sidekick Georgie O'Connor. They were two of the best players going. But they came at a price on account of being a heap of trouble.

'How come you missed the minibus?'

'It's a long story. Give's the fare.'

'Tell me the story first.'

The story was typical. Ginger and Georgie had gone to the pictures the night before with some pals, to this plush eight-screen cinema. They got fed up with the film they were watching and went on a tour of the others.

Someone complained about kids running wild, chasing from one film to the next and jumping over seats like they were hurdles in the Olympics. The staff went in search and it ended up as a game of hide-and-seek.

They all escaped except Ginger who got caught. He ended up in deep trouble as one of the pals had set off the fire alarm and the whole cinema had to be evacuated. Ginger's da was called for, dragged out of the nearest pub. Ginger was brought home by the scruff of the neck and told that as punishment he wouldn't be playing for Riverside next day. But he got out through a window with his football gear. He made a run for the minibus but was too late.

'Can I have the fare now?'

I thought it over. If this were to be the future, I'd never be rid of Riverside. Still, I gave him the fare and told him to get lost.

Later I went up the town to pass an hour.

Who did I meet but the Captain. Now that I was no longer actively involved in the campaign I could afford to be seen talking to him. I crossed the road to enquire how life was treating the old bones. He had been shopping for pork chops and broccoli. We sat on a bench, had a chat and watched the world of Bray pass by. Talking to him head-to-head he didn't seem loopy in the least. He was perfectly at ease and made sense.

'Damn tyrant, that Mrs O'Leary. She thinks I'm a hothead. That I'll cause too much trouble. Her! Who does she think she is?'

'Probably Joan of Arc on a bad day.'

'I know bringing the sword to the building site probably wasn't a very bright idea. And charging the workers was even worse. But the thought of demolishing that defenceless school irritates me. I feel for the place. It is part of my heritage, part of who I am.'

'You didn't half do a good job with those tapes. We heard them again last night. They worked a treat.'

He smiled. 'Yes, I'm proud of that. And I'll come up with some equally good headline grabber. Some other ruse. But I won't be telling Mrs O'Leary.'

Although he had called Mrs O'Leary a 'damn tyrant' he also had a few kind words to say about her. He made the point she was the only councillor to try and stop the demolition of the old school. All the others had turned a blind eye! He was no fool either; he knew Mrs O'Leary with her council-chamber connections was probably the only person who had an earthly of saving it. But could she out-fox the developers?

I asked him how the sword was getting on.

'It has a new home.'

'Where?'

'For over a year I've been attempting to trace the true descendants of Iron Fist Jones. The sword is on its way to them right now.'

'That's cool. Maybe they will let you

parade it once a year.'

'Don't think so.'

'Why not?'

'They live in the wilds of Canada. Goose Bay to be exact. Couldn't have picked a better name. The area covers hundreds of miles. Frozen waste. Nothing but ice and snow. And the odd grizzly. The descendants of Iron Fist arrived there in the late 1860s. They felt like a change of location. Maybe they were pushed.'

I often heard my da say: 'People move on.' Now I knew what he meant.

We chatted a few more minutes, mainly about Monday's four-o'clock protest. I didn't say I wasn't going to turn up.

I left the Captain in a sombre mood. He knew he was on his last campaign. The sword was gone and the old school wouldn't be long in following. Not to Goose Bay but, alas, to some landfill site in the obscurity of the Wicklow countryside.

Deep down he knew he was fighting a lost cause. But he'd keep a stiff upper lip. That's what he was about. He wasn't a quitter. He'd fight to the bitter end.

When I got home I gradually began to wonder how the U-12s had done against Ballybrack. After spending so many years managing the team in the past it was only natural to be curious as to how they had got on. Football had been such a vital part of my life that it was hard to erase it completely. I'd always have football on my mind. I'd always be checking results, league tables and the latest transfer news. There wouldn't be a match shown on TV that I wouldn't watch.

I'm a true 'nutter'.

I was outside sitting on the garden wall when Baby Joe McCann and Pee Wee Flood came up along the estate. They were swinging their football bags in a carefree way. Just by looking I knew they had won the match. But I asked anyway.

'We won 2-1. Pee Wee here got the first, Dave Doherty got the other. He went up for a corner and headed the ball into the net. The goal-keeper hadn't a chance. Illie stood in his way but the referee didn't notice so the goal stood. The Ballybrack lads weren't long telling Illie to go back to Romania. But Harry Hennessy told them to get lost. We'll stuff them in the Park too. Can't wait to get them in Bray. Mr Glynn says we're gettin' better by the day.'

'What did you do today, Jimmy?'

'Not much.'

'Miss the team?'

'A little.'

'Heard about your job. A newspaper reporter, that's cool! Superman was one in his spare time. You'll come to the Park and do some reportin' on us, won't you?'

'Sure.'

'By the way,' added Pee Wee, 'Ginger Mullin told me to tell you the money you gave him for the bus fare was nothing but rotten bad luck.'

'What do you mean?'

'The goal Ballybrack scored was an own goal. Ginger thumped the ball into his own net. He played brutal. Wished he had missed the match altogether.'

And that was what I'd miss about Riverside most. Not the football, but the hopelessly crazy fun-filled moments that made our lives so splendidly carefree. That would be impossible to replace.

I went down to the seafront, bought a paper and turned to the sports columns. Flintstone flashed by on his Eddie Merckx racer. He hadn't time to stop, just gave a wave and peddled like mad to meet up with his pals from Bray Wheelers and whatever race was in the offing.

As always, I turned to the results section to see how Forest Albion did. They had won 2-nil away to Scunthorpe. Though it was only early season I knew Scunthorpe's form from the previous season had been good. For Forest Albion to beat them 2-nil away was pretty impressive stuff. There was no match report on the page, just the result and the names of the goal-scorers. Patrice (the star of Chippy's 'Samba Soccer' school) had scored the winning goal.

On another page the teams from the various divisions were listed, with marks out of ten for performance. Surprise, surprise, Chippy's name was included! He had got seven out of ten for performance. That was good. Only two others got more, one of whom was Patrice.

Chippy had made his first-team league debut!

There had been no talk in advance that it was on the cards. It had come like a bolt from the blue.

Excited by Chippy's success I realised I had my first scoop. I'd do an article on him for the *Bray People*. Who better than myself? We had grown up together, played football together, even fallen out together. I had it all, plus a signed photo of him when he played Schoolboy for Ireland. Soon as I walked into the office on Monday morning I'd sit at whatever desk they assigned me, take out the pen and paper, and get cracking writing the schoolboy soccer scoop of the year. I wasn't nervous about the job any longer. Instead, I felt over the moon. I couldn't wait to get started.

On the way home I met several Riverside players. Once home I got on the phone to Mr Glynn and Harry Hennessy.

I had the same news for them all.

'Hear about Chippy?'

'No.'

'Get the *News of the World*. Look at the football, where it lists the teams from the lower divisions. Chippy made his league debut for Forest Albion yesterday.'

'Is it in any of the other papers?'

'Should be. But it's definitely in the *News of the World*.'

And it *was* in most of the other papers.

There was a match report in one. Chippy didn't get an individual mention, but his name was listed

Thanks to Chippy's debut, there was a big run on Sunday papers that day. One of the few to miss out was Flintstone. He got back late from his stint with Bray Wheelers and all the shops were closed. But he wasn't too upset. He knew where all the unsold newspapers were collected (from a skip beside a petrol station on the edge of Bray). He went there with a flashlight and helped himself to a copy of each available paper. When he got back home he cut out the bits with Chippy's name. The rest he left in some oul' wan's dustbin.

I remember my ma saying there were no trumpets blown when I was born. It was the same with Chippy's first-team debut for Forest Albion. There were no fanfares, no fuss. Not even his parents knew until it was over. Not that Chippy would have wanted it that way. He was not one for turning down the limelight. But he had no choice. He had only got the call that morning.

'Be on the team bus.'

And he was.

On arrival: 'Tog out. You're playing.'

Chippy had just about beaten me to the punch. It wouldn't be until Monday that I would become a junior soccer reporter. Chippy always bettered me no matter what. This time was no different.

I was glad for him.

13 The Last Hurrah

My first job as a trainee newspaper reporter was to go to the shop for a carton of milk and make the tea. In between times, I sat behind a desk and twiddled my thumbs while they worked at lightning speed typing reports (on computers) and getting all sorts of information over the phone. Editor Fred wasn't there that morning. His assistant listened to my idea for a feature about Chippy and said to wait until he came in and then run it past him.

About one o'clock the activity died down and most of them went for lunch before going off to follow up leads for the week's news. That left me and this other chap alone in the office. His job was to answer the phone and either take messages or divert the call to the appropriate mobile. I sat and looked at the clock, watching the arms crawl around to four pm.

At twenty minutes past the hour, a call came through saying there was trouble brewing at the top end of Main Street. The other chap told me to go and investigate 'the disturbance'. He'd locate a senior reporter and send him after me.

'What do I do?'

'Just make notes. Ask someone what it's about? See what's happening, who's there.'

'I don't think I should go,' I told him.

'What do you mean?'

'Could I okay it with the Boss first?'

'He won't be back, not until later. Look, I can't go. I have to man the office. You're the only one.'

I knew of course what the rumpus was about. The *Save the Old School* protest. The Phantom Army was on the rampage.

'If the trouble is what I think it is, I have a problem.'

'Like what?'

'The Boss told me to keep away. He told me not to get involved.'

He plainly thought I was some kind of half wit. 'You don't have to get involved. Just find out what's going on.'

'Can you cover for me with the Boss?'

'Get moving!'

'What about the Boss?'

'I'll deal with that.'

I left and went straight to the old school. I knew it had to be the centre of the trouble. And I was spot on.

There wasn't just trouble. There was a mini riot!

I hadn't been prepared for a new development. The old school was gone! The workers had had inside information about the protest and had demolished it at first light. The sausage factory and fire-extinguisher plant were also gone, everything taken away on a fleet of red and white lorries and dumped in the middle of nowhere. The only person to witness the destruction had been a sleepy-eyed milkman.

The sudden rush of rage I felt took me by surprise.

Okay, the old school hadn't been much of a building but it had stood for nearly two hundred years. Even if it wasn't part of *our* culture (whatever that is) it was part of the life of Bray. It could have been saved. It would have mixed in with the new development. But no! For the sake of the small amount of space it occupied it had to be flattened. It would have meant the loss of another shop or an extra office.

I didn't really blame the developers. This was *business*. Culture and heritage and the past are all very well – in their place, which isn't anywhere near where there were millions at stake.

With the old school gone, Mrs O'Leary and the Captain could have called off the march. They didn't. They had marched on the site, sixty strong, placards held high, chanting their slogans. It was to be a peaceful, dignified protest. Absolutely no violence of any kind.

Growler Hughes was up front with Victor, Henry and Flintstone. Sheila had brought along her vampire friends. They had multiplied – there were now 14 of them. The rank and file had expanded too (though none of my U-12 showed up) and the whole turnout looked very impressive. The Captain had brought along a megaphone. He meant to reinstate himself as leader, with or without Mrs O'Leary's approval.

The small army of protestors paraded

along Main Street chanting their slogans. It took them ten minutes to reach the site but as they neared it the chanting turned into gasps of disbelief. There wasn't as much as a trace of rubble where the school, the sausage factory and the extinguisher plant had been. All that was left was fresh air and a nice touch of September sunshine.

That section of the site had been hurriedly cordoned off with plywood hoarding. There was a wide entrance, strung across which were some of the workers. The front of the protest procession now stood facing them.

There was a short standoff. Mrs O'Leary began to conduct them, right hand clawing the air, in *We Shall Overcome*. Those at the back who couldn't see what was going on joined the singing and began to press forward.

Could it last?

Captain Darley was the first to crack. He was absolutely livid. He felt highly insulted, grievously wronged. He was beyond the reach of reason. It was time to act! He shoved Mrs O'Leary aside, gripped the megaphone to his lips, and roared, 'Charge!'

There was a surge forward and the colourful mix of adults, vampires and an assortment of children swept by the cordon of workers in their white safety helmets.

I arrived at this point.

Mrs O'Leary hadn't intended to get caught up in the action. But the crowd behind her propelled her forward with irresistible force and she was soon in the thick of the fray. Three white helmets clattered to the ground from the force of her handbag. She and the Captain flayed all around them until the last of the white helmets retreated into the gigantic crater at the front of the site where the underground car park was being built.

The protesters gathered in a circle before it. When they had finished *We Shall Overcome,* Sheila and the vampires struck up a song used by South American revolutionaries during the time of Che Guevara and Fidel Castro.

By the time the third protest song got under way the white helmets reappeared from the car park. This time they were in the company of some blue helmets, with a few

red helmets thrown in. No one had a clue what the colours signified except they were definitely connected with the development and therefore on the other side.

A further standoff developed.

The protesters, now on their seventh song, sang with such gusto that they could be heard as far away as the Town Hall where about twenty Spanish students were attending an exhibition. They made a sudden beeline towards the source of the singing and were absolutely thrilled to join in and be a part of the protest.

I kept my distance, not wanting to get involved for fear I'd get into trouble and lose my brand-new job. Okay, the chap in the office had told me to go to Main Street but the real boss had warned me to keep clear of the protest. I'd go by him. If the senior reporter didn't come soon, I'd go back to the office and say nothing much had happened. I wouldn't mention any names. I reminded myself that I had been hired as a junior *soccer* reporter. My scoop for the week would be Chippy making his first-team debut for Forest Albion.

Just as I thought that everyone was going to stand there forever confronting each other, one of the red helmets approached Mrs O'Leary. Whatever he said made her feel so mad that she took a swipe at him with her handbag. He ducked and grabbed her by the arm. That was probably something he shouldn't have done.

The Captain rushed forward, raised his arm and shouted into the megaphone, 'Attack!'

There was an instant surge forward, followed by much pushing and shoving, with the men in the multi-coloured helmets attempting to come to grips with the protestors and push them off the site. But there were too many of them, the worst being the nippers who could dart through their legs. That's until the police arrived in numbers and soon had them under control..

I watched it all from a new vantage point – a garden wall just across the road. I wasn't worried about getting clear of the clogged site and the crowded access streets. Or of being picked up by the police.

I had my escape route planned.

I just walked to the door marked **Exit Point** and into the small cul-de-sac where Captain Darley's bubble car was parked. No doubt within minutes he would come charging through it and make his escape.

I didn't wait around to witness it.

When I got back to the office, Fred had arrived. He was talking on his phone and to one of senior reporters in the office at the same time. He stopped when I came in.

'Jimmy, give Joe your notes.'

'I didn't take any.'

'What?'

Everyone in the office stared at me.

'You mean to say you were sent down to report an incident and you've come back with nothing.'

'You said I wasn't to get involved.'

He gave me a baffled look and turned back to Joe.

'Get down there straightaway and find out what's been happening. Jimmy here can fill you in on the background later.'

I stood there feeling two foot high.

'Well, young Quinn. Not a great start to your career.'

'But you said...'

'Jimmy! Get yourself sorted out. Writing articles on lost causes is one thing. But when you're sent along to report a near riot on the Main Street, that's *news* and you come back with it.'

I didn't know what I expected at that stage. Instant dismissal. Demotion to permanent tea-maker.

But he was smiling at me.

'I don't think you'll make that mistake twice ... Ned here was telling me you wanted to do a story about Chippy. That's a great scoop. And the fact that you found it in the small print shows real interest in your work. Now, get the riot down on paper for Joe and then you can go on to the Chippy story.'

So ended my first day.

Anxiety.

Indecision.

Worry.

Mortification.

Fear.

Soaring ecstasy.

Someone once wrote about an actor whose performance ran through the whole gamut of emotions from A to B.

I managed A to Z.

14 Exit Point

Later that roller-coaster day, Victor and Henry came calling.

'We've bad news.'

'How bad?'

'The *Save the School* campaign is finished.'

'That's hardly news. What would be the point now that the school is gone?'

'There's more. Mrs O'Leary, the Captain and Growler got arrested. And your girl-friend, as well as some of her weirdo pals. They were all brought in a police van to a special sittin' of Bray Court. They were bound to the peace and told not to go within a mile of the building site until the job is finished. If they do they'll be sent to jail.'

'That's rough.'

'Pity Mrs O'Leary wasn't sent to jail though. That would have been some laugh.'

'She's still in trouble.'

'What do you mean?'

'Well, Bray Council meetings are held in the Town Hall and that's only a hundred yards from the site. It means she won't be able to attend any Council meetings.'

That would be the best news her fellow councillors would get all year. Or at least until she had talked her way out of the ban.

To Victor, I said, 'You were lucky not to get picked up. I thought one of the garda had your cap from the time before.'

'Yeah. It was Hot Pursuit. He gave it back to me and told me to go home and stay out of trouble.'

I remembered Hot Pursuit, the garda who was always in pursuit of whatever he was supposed to be in pursuit of without ever actually catching it. Maybe he was letting whatever he caught off with a warning.

'You deserted us, you know,' said Victor.

I couldn't lie to Victor.

'It's my new job. Reporters are not supposed to get mixed up in causes.'

'I suppose so.'

He didn't sound angry. Just resigned.

We shook hands and parted.

I felt sorry for Growler. A little. I wondered if his court appearance would affect his prospect of a bank job.

Actually he didn't get a bank job but not because of that. Apparently arctic winds were blowing through the world of sub-prime loans and the banks were getting less keen on lending large sums of money to men in string vests with no fixed assets. They were cutting back on everything and that included Growler.

Whenever I thought about it, I wondered why I, who knew nothing about high finance, could see that sub-prime was daft while all the high-flyers didn't.

But of course, I had one great advantage.

I had Da.

I also felt sorry for the Captain. I never saw him again. He left Bray and was said to have been sighted in the wilds of Connemara. Though sometimes it was in the foothills of the Mournes or some suburb of Dublin where he was reputed to have an elderly sister. In any event, he's probably in one place or the other.

I didn't feel sorry for Sheila. She disappeared off the scene some time after. She was said to have gone to London.

The holiday that the councillors of Bray had looked forward to was short-lived. Mrs O'L soon got back to the Town Hall to continue her crusades. Though she never did become Lord Mayor.

The new shopping centre didn't have much luck either. It got caught up in the collapse of the Celtic Tiger and became the hole-in-the-ground Mark II.

Chippy went from strength to strength.

When I walked through the door marked **Exit Point,** I had known, as surely as I had ever known anything, that it was a turning point. There was no going back. It made me feel down in the dumps. I was no longer a kid. I was now in the adult world.

What else can I say? Except perhaps say a word of thanks to those who have taken an interest in Riverside. It meant a lot to me too.

Like I've written somewhere before:

And so it was the end.

So long.

Farewell.

Goodbye.

The End

Jimmy

Chippy

Mad Victor

Mad Henry

Flintstone

Growler

Peter Regan

Riverside: The Street League

Mrs O'Leary has a GREAT IDEA. Start a street-
league! To keep all the tea-leaves around the
place out of trouble. And get a little publicity –
which might come in handy in view of
impending Council elections.
Riverside to a man – or a U-14 – rise to the
challenge. Which team will bring home the
Brenda O'Leary Perpetual Cup?
But, of course, football is not the only thing
on their minds. Chippy has his gran to worry
about. Jimmy has to sort out his da, write a
book, and dream about the beautiful Heather
McFadden. Mad Victor has his own ideas;
especially where Mrs O'Leary is concerned …

Peter Regan

Riverside: The Croke Park Conspiracy

It's the witching hour of night and two
shadowy figures are stealing across the
People's Park.
One of them produces a bushman saw and
they start sawing. A few minutes later, the
skinny GAA goal-posts are in the river.
Naturally there's blue murder and Mrs O'Leary
(now Councillor O'Leary) springs into action.
Riverside Boys v the GAA is on!
In between skirmishes, Chippy has a great
idea, Brains O'Mahony has another, and Mad
Victor and Mad Henry see a bit of the world.
Jimmy has something else on his mind – who,
in the absence of his masterpiece, *Forlorn Love*,
will win the Book-of-the-Year Award!

Peter Regan

Riverside: City Slickers

After a showdown with Chippy who won the
Book-of-the-Year Award with *his* idea,
Jimmy gets to keep the prize for a year and
fifty quid. New boots *and* a computer
(if he can learn to use it – Brains O'Mahony
says it's banjaxed).
But Mrs O'Leary is on the warpath. Who's been
slagging her by writing on the walls? Who's
trampling on the flower-beds on Bray sea
front? She suspects Mad Victor and
she's out to get him.
That's if she can spare the time.
She's started a campaign to reclaim the
Town Hall from McDonald's. So she rustles a
cow and sets off up Main Street …

Peter Regan

Riverside: The London Trip

'Flintstone has disappeared! When he reappears
(policeman in tow) he's minus his bag. And
we're only at Euston station, and the Great
London Soccer Weekend hasn't even started.
Up and down escalators. More bags nicked.
Missed connections. Frayed nerves. And when
we get to play match number one we're greeted
by a geezer with Santa Claus whiskers and a
striped rugby-club tie.
Rugby! Compromise: soccer first half, rugby
next half. We flatten them and scarper.
But the big news is Chippy. Is he in trouble?
PS. Cock-ups courtesy of Harry Hennessy, last
seen disappearing at Crewe station in search of
a strong cup of tea …'

117

Peter Regan

Riverside: Loot!

Mad Victor, Flintstone and Jimmy take up local
history and make a find that completely
changes their lives. Now they have new
worries. Where did it – the find – come from?
Can they hide it so it won't be found? Should
they keep it? Tell someone?
Will anyone claim it?
Meanwhile, there's Da (the Road Runner) to
contend with, plus fire, horse-racing, voodoo,
suspected shop-lifting, arrests …
Mrs O'Leary comes up with a startling idea
that could set Jimmy off on a new career.
That is if he can keep out of the clutches of
Oul' Black Eyes …

Peter Regan

Riverside: Dynamo Rouge

Want to be a football manager?
It's not all it's cracked up to be.
Jimmy Flynn, 14, and manager of Dynamo
Rouge U-10, has a few words of advice.
'Among other things you have to learn to talk and
chew gum at the same time. I was so good at it
most of the kids thought I was Alex Ferguson.'
Chippy has lost interest. But Flintstone is Team
Trainer and Mad (camcorder) Victor Official
Recorder. Can he keep out of trouble with
Mrs O'Leary? Can Terry O'Sullivan escape
the clutches of the law and Bray Urban Council?
It all leads to Dynamo Rouge being arrested
en masse and Terry, Mad Victor and Mad
Henry vanishing to Birmingham …

Peter Regan

Riverside: Scout

Jimmy just has to lay hands on a Tottenham
Hotspur scout. Otherwise Georgie and Ginger
are going to defect. And the new Riverside
U-10s will sink before they swim.
Chippy has an idea (well he would, wouldn't
he?): ask Brains O'Mahony. And it turns out
Brains O'Mahony *can* help. But he wants
Jimmy to do a favour for a friend of his. It
involves Da. Which, given how things are
between Jimmy and Da most of the time, could
be more than a bit tricky …

Peter Regan

Riverside: Setbacks

Victor and Henry are home and though Jimmy
and Chippy and Flintstone and Catho rally
around, it's touch and go. Especially with
Mrs O'Leary on A-Alert, waiting to catch and
reshape them For Their Own Good.
Meanwhile, will the U-10s hold on to second
place in the league? Can they?
Georgie and Ginger are acting up – *Where's the
Tottenham scout?* Christmas is coming and
Christmas, as Jimmy notes, is a bad time for
managers, what with bugs laying low key
players, pitches under snow, and goal-scoring
mega-Yetis looming out of the blizzards.
Nothing but setbacks. Wanted a miracle.
Enter an angel disguised as Hot Pursuit ...

Peter Regan

Riverside: The Curse

'After all the upset we had at Farmer Joe's
over Christmas, you'd think that we
(me, Flintstone and the U-10s) could settle
down to playing soccer.
What a hope!
First it's Mad Victor who's been hit by the
movie-making bug and wants me (the only
writer he knows) to come up with a story.
Then Pee Wee meets an 'oul lad who stuffs him
full of rubbish about a curse on the river
(our pitch is right beside it).
That really hits the spot with the U-10s.
Panic sets in.
Meanwhile Chippy weasels his way back into
the team as trainer. Will I be sidelined?'

Peter Regan

Riverside: The Movie

Summer!
And it looks like being long and hot.
Time for lazy, hazy days thinks Jimmy.
How wrong can anyone get?
First Victor keeps nagging away about the
super film he's about to make. He loads Jimmy
down with acres of material and wants
a script by wireless.
Then Georgie and Ginger want action on the
soccer front and won't take 'No' for an answer.
Hardly leaves time to find out what Mad Henry
and Chippy are up to …

Peter Regan

Riverside: The Spy

Mandy!
Having nearly run her down on Flintstone's
Eddie Merckx racing bike, Jimmy is snared
'hook, line and sinker'.
He is stunned to find out that the most beautiful
girl in Bray wants to follow the fortunes of the
Riverside U-11 team he manages.
Team morale rises no end!
But a girl like Mandy likes to be at the centre of
things. In particular, she likes to hear the
team secrets.
Meanwhile Gypsy and Tootsie are
causing ripples …

Peter Regan

Riverside: Spring Fever

The good news! Jimmy's da has done a FÁS
course and joined the bricklaying fraternity.
The sound of horses' hooves (carrying his
money) no longer dominates family life.
The bad news! The Christmas 'mocks' (for
Leaving Cert) are looming up and most of
Jimmy's year haven't got a clue. Maths and
Science are Double Dutch.
But more good news! Growler Hughes just
happens to be passing an open door in school
and the exam papers just happen to be lying
around and the teacher just happens
to be missing...
They all know it won't help come June...
June? A lifetime away!

Riverside: Samba Soccer

Come summer! Come Chippy!
The bad news: Aston Villa have let him go.
The good news: Forest Albion have signed him up.
As usual, he's full of plans. The kind that make
your eyes light up with € signs.
He's going to have a five-day soccer school for
the Bray nippers. Not just any old school.
A *Samba Soccer* school!
Jimmy says he's too busy to help – Leaving Cert.
He's roped in anyway, and so is Flintstone with
his new messenger-boy bike, which has a
history that brings tears to Mrs O'Leary's eyes.
Talking of Mrs O'L, when news seeps out about
the advent of Brazilians in Bray, even she wants
to get in on the act …

126